MISTER MOMBOO'S HAT

Story by Ralph Leemis
Pictures by Jeni Bassett

COBBLEHILL BOOKS   Dutton New York

To my father, who
gave me the hat from his head—R.L.

To Justin Leemis—J.B.

Text copyright © 1991 by Ralph Leemis
Illustrations copyright © 1991 by Jeni Bassett Leemis
Library of Congress Cataloging-in-Publication Data

Leemis, Ralph.
Mister Momboo's hat / story by Ralph Leemis ; pictures by Jeni Bassett.
p.   cm.
Summary: An elephant's hat takes off on adventures of its own.
ISBN 0-525-65045-8
[1. Hats—Fiction.   2. Stories in rhyme.]   I. Bassett, Jeni, ill.   II. Title.
PZ8.3.L5Mi   1991
[E]—dc20   90-34397   CIP   AC

Published in the United States by Cobblehill Books,
an affiliate of Dutton Children's Books,
a division of Penguin Books USA Inc.
Designed by Charlotte Staub
Printed in Hong Kong
First Edition   10 9 8 7 6 5 4 3 2 1

Mister Momboo had a very fine hat,

but the wind came along and took care of that.

The hat flew along till it came to a boy,

who thought that it made a most wonderful toy.

The hat stayed behind when the boy went inside,

then left once again . . .

. . . when it went for a ride.

A frog was surprised by the traveling hat,

then was chased down a hill by a curious cat.

The hat was a boat as it floated away

and soon it became the catch of the day.

The hat was a gift to a friend who had none,

then kept a horse cool in the heat of the sun.

In autumn the hat was no longer needed,

but helped watch a garden just recently seeded.

In springtime two robins then thought it was best

to turn Mister Momboo's hat . . .

. . . into a nest.